KU-723-044

FIFE EDUCATION
COMMITTEE

KING'S ROAD P. SCHOOL

ROSYTH

ISBN 0 86163 078 5

© Award Publications Limited 1983
Spring House, Spring Place
London N.W. 5

Printed in Belgium

SNOW WHITE
AND
THE SEVEN DWARFS

Illustrated by RENE CLOKE

AWARD PUBLICATIONS — LONDON

SNOW WHITE AND THE SEVEN DWARFS

There was once a Queen who pricked her finger as she sat sewing one snowy day.

As she looked at the drop of blood which fell from her hand, she said:

"How I would like a little daughter with skin as pure as the snow, lips as red as blood and hair as black as the window frame."

And when her little girl was born that is just how she looked, so she was named Snow White.

But, before long, the Queen died and the King married again.

The new Queen was very beautiful but very vain and she would look in her Magic Mirror and ask:

"Mirror, mirror
on the wall,
Who is the fairest
of us all?"

and was very pleased when the Magic Mirror answered:

"Thou, O Queen,
art the fairest
of them all."

But as Snow White grew up, she became more and more beautiful and the Queen felt very jealous and angry.

One day she asked her mirror,

"Mirror, mirror on the wall,
Who is the fairest of us all?"

and was furious at the reply:

"Snow White is the fairest of you all."

She told a huntsman to take the little girl into the forest and kill her.

But the huntsman was a kind man and decided not to do as he was ordered.

He took Snow White into the forest and left her there, warning her not to go back to the Palace.

Snow White was very frightened at first but the animals she met were friendly and she wandered happily in the forest until evening.

It was growing dusk
when Snow White came to a
little cottage amongst the
trees.

"Perhaps someone will let me spend the
night here," said Snow White.

It looked such a friendly little cottage that
she walked boldly up the path and tapped on
the door.

No one answered, so Snow White, finding
the door unlocked, stepped inside.

7

The cottage was just as pretty inside as outside.

Snow White found seven little chairs drawn up to the table and seven little beds neatly arranged in a row.

"This cottage must belong to seven very small people," thought Snow White, "perhaps they will be kind to a little girl."

She took a tiny piece of bread from each plate and a tiny piece of cheese.

Then she took a sip of milk from each mug and, feeling weary after the long day in the forest, she curled up on one of the little beds and fell asleep.

Now the cottage belonged to seven dwarfs, who spent their days digging for gold and precious stones in the mountains nearby.

Every morning they went forth with their picks and shovels and worked all day, filling their sacks with gold and jewels.

And every evening they lighted their
lanterns and came back to their cottage in the
forest.

When they arrived that night, they saw at once that somebody had been tasting their supper.

They looked around and soon discovered Snow White asleep in bed.

"How beautiful she is!" whispered one.

"Shall we wake her?" asked another.

Their voices roused Snow White and she sat up in bed, looking in astonishment at the seven little dwarfs.

When she told them her story, they very
kindly said that she could stay with them in
the cottage for as long as she liked.

Snow White was very helpful to the dwarfs and kept their cottage clean and tidy.

She cooked meals for them and told them bed-time stories.

All the little animals who lived in the forest came to visit her, so she was never lonely when the dwarfs were away.

The jealous Queen now
asked her Magic Mirror who
was the fairest in the land
and was amazed when the
Mirror answered:

"In the forest,
with seven dwarfs small,
Lives Snow White, the
fairest of you all."

The Queen, who was really a witch, made
her wicked plans.

First she turned herself into an old
woman, then she collected a basket of dainty
ribbons and laces and set off for the forest.

She soon found the dwarfs' cottage and knocked at the door.

Snow White peeped from the window.

"I have some pretty things for sale," said the old woman, "see how well this ribbon would lace your bodice."

The dwarfs had told Snow White not to open the door to anyone, but the laces and ribbons looked so pretty that she forgot their warning.

She let the old woman lace her bodice
with the bright ribbon.

But the Queen laced it so tightly that
Snow White fell to the ground faint and
breathless.

The Queen hurried home and was puzzled
when the mirror told her that Snow White
was still the most beautiful in the land, for she
did not know that the dwarfs had returned
early, cut the laces from Snow White's bodice
and saved her life.

The wicked Queen
put on another
disguise and filled a
tray with some pretty
things.

She tapped at the cottage window and
called out:

"Would you like to buy some pretty
trinkets? See, here is such a dainty comb."

"I must not open the door," answered
Snow White.

"No need," replied the Queen, "Just let me
set this comb in your hair for you."

The old woman sounded so kind that Snow White leant from the window and allowed her to place the comb in her lovely black hair.

But the comb was poisoned and Snow White dropped senseless to the ground.

When the dwarfs arrived home, they snatched the comb from Snow White's head and she quickly recovered.

The Magic Mirror still declared that Snow White was the fairest of them all, so the Queen thought out another wicked plot.

She took a rosy apple and poisoned it on one side only; then she dressed herself in another cloak and hat and painted her face so that Snow White should not recognize her.

But Snow White had learned to be very careful.

"Your apples look delicious," she told the old woman, "but I have been warned to buy nothing at the door."

"It's quite safe," laughed the old woman, "I will bite this side and you can bite the other."

Seeing that the apple did the old woman no harm, Snow White took it and bit the other side and at once fell down dead.

The dwarfs were horrified when they found her and did all they could to revive her, but nothing would bring her back to life.

They were very
sorrowful and the next day
they made a beautiful glass
coffin and placed Snow
White in it with many
flowers around her.

They carried it to the top of the mountain
and kept watch there.

One day, a prince came riding by and
seeing the lovely girl, he at once fell in love
with her and persuaded the dwarfs to carry
Snow White back to his palace.

At last the Dwarfs agreed, but they
stumbled on the way and the piece of apple
was shaken from Snow White's throat.

"She lives, she lives!" cried the dwarfs as Snow White sat up and looked around her.

"Come to my palace and marry me," begged the Prince. Snow White agreed for she loved the Prince instantly and there was soon a very grand wedding.

All the seven dwarfs were there and gave
Snow White and the Prince some beautiful
presents from their store of
treasure.

The wicked
Queen grew tired
of questioning her
Magic Mirror and
turned its face to
the wall!